D1367180

My Easter Story

Maria Hoskins

ILLUSTRATED BY

Rex DeLoney

C&V 4 SEASONS PUBLISHING CO.

International Standard Book Number (ISBN) 978-0-9864036-5-1
Library of Congress Control Number: 2016919627

Cataloging-in-Publication data

Names: Hoskins, Maria, author. | Deloney, Rex, illustrator.
Title: My Easter story / written by Maria Hoskins ; illustrated by Rex Deloney.
Description: Mayflower, AR: C & V 4 Seasons Publishing Co., 2017.
Identifiers: ISBN 978-0-9864036-5-1 | LCCN 2016919627
Summary: A child tells her own story of Easter morning, including breakfast with her family, a speech at
church, and the story of Christ.
Subjects: LCSH Easter stories. | African American children--Juvenile fiction. | Family—Juvenile fiction. | BI-
SAC JUVENILE FICTION / Holidays & Celebrations / Easter & Lent
Classification: LCC PZ7.H79335 Ea 2017 | DDC [E]—dc23

www.seasons2dream.com

Easter

Month _____ Date _____ Year _____

I attended Church at _____

What I liked best about Easter was

_____

_____

_____

_____

_____

_____

_____

Easter means I can see the sun shining so bright that it makes me squint my eyes; I can feel the fresh air breeze touching my skin, and the air smells like grandma's fresh washed laundry.

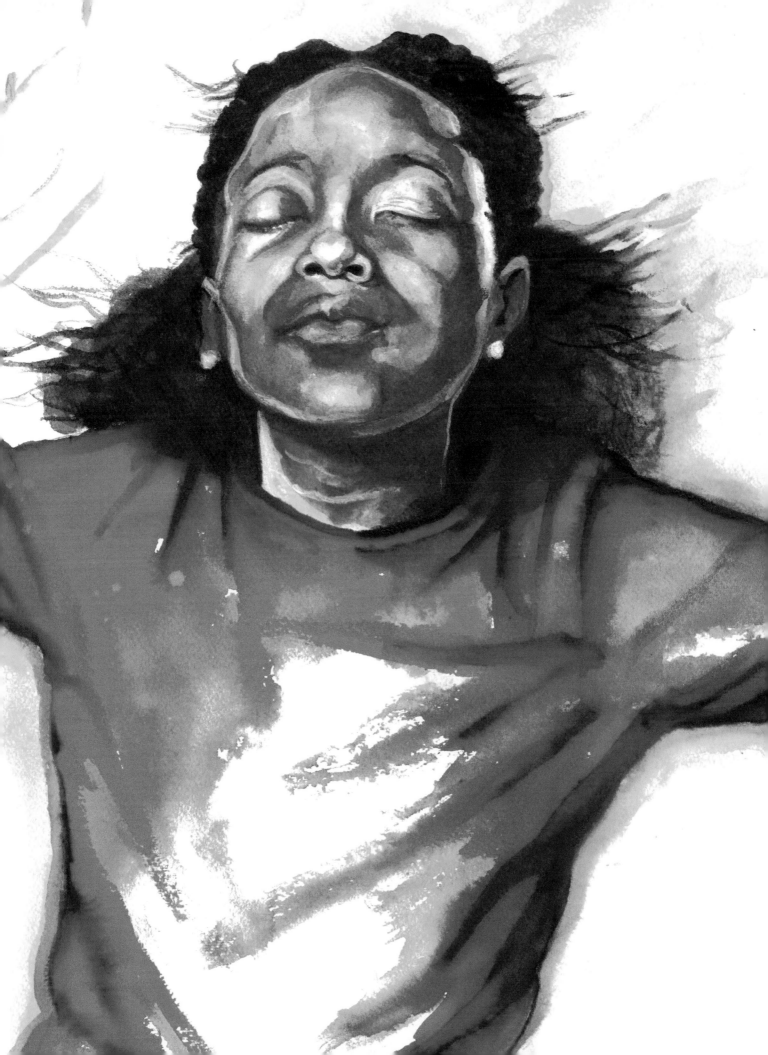

Easter means we get up early and go shopping for groceries and new clothes for Easter Sunday! First, we go shopping for new Easter clothes! I get a new dress, a brand new pair of shoes, get my hair done, and all of the extras! After shopping for new Easter clothes, momma buys groceries for grandma's Sunday Easter breakfast and our after church meal.

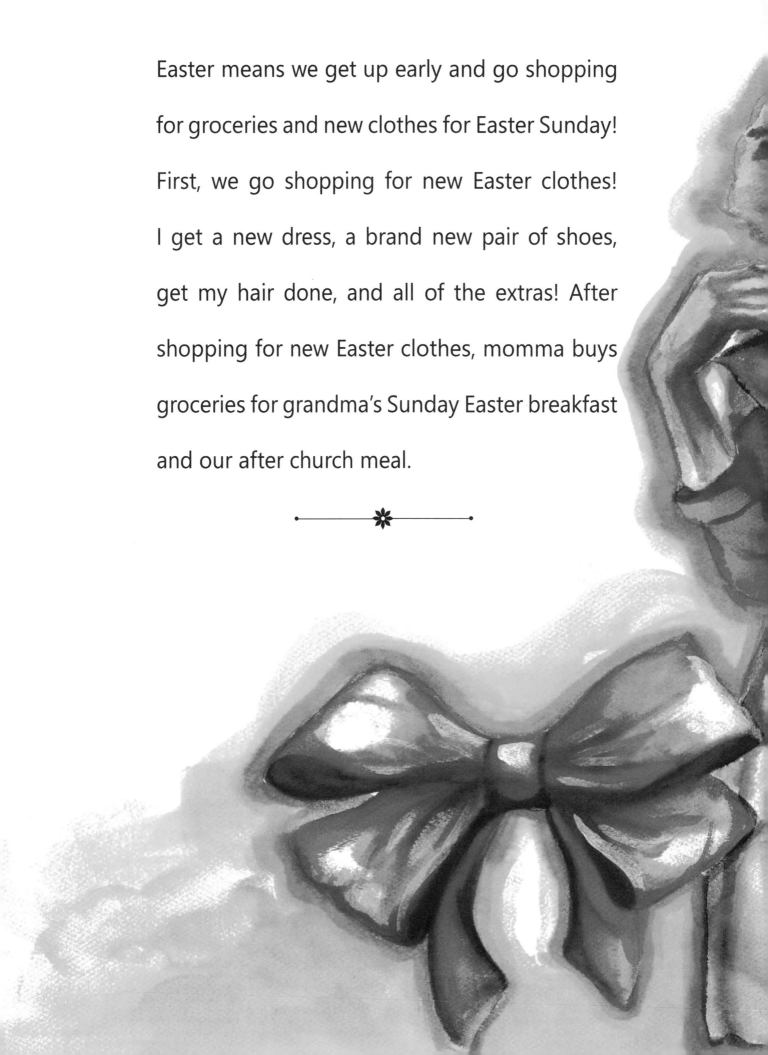

After all of the house chores are done on Saturday afternoon, we get to color eggs for the church Easter Egg Hunt. I love coloring eggs for Easter; I make yellow, red, pink, blue, and green eggs—a rainbow of Easter eggs.

We get up early Easter Sunday morning for a big breakfast. Yum, grandma and momma make pancakes, eggs, biscuits, bacon, sausage, grits, fried potatoes, fruit, and hot chocolate. Yummy, so good!

✻

After breakfast, I get to put on my pretty new blue Easter dress, a new bow for my hair, and my new red shoes; I love my new red shoes! Now, off to church we go.

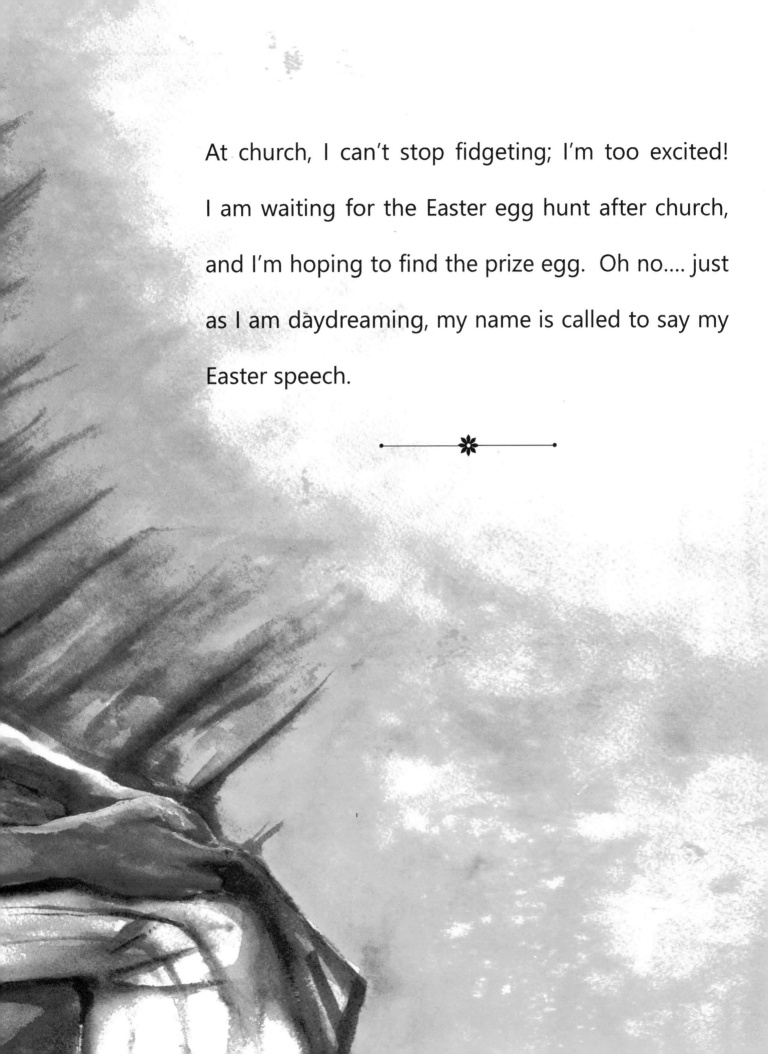

At church, I can't stop fidgeting; I'm too excited! I am waiting for the Easter egg hunt after church, and I'm hoping to find the prize egg. Oh no.... just as I am daydreaming, my name is called to say my Easter speech.

Everyone is so quiet, I think to myself; can they see my legs shaking? I try not to look at anyone. Mother said I cannot look at the paper the speech is written on; I must know it by memory. I say my speech very fast.

Today is Easter;
I want to say,
Happy Easter Day!

I did good! I did not forget my speech.

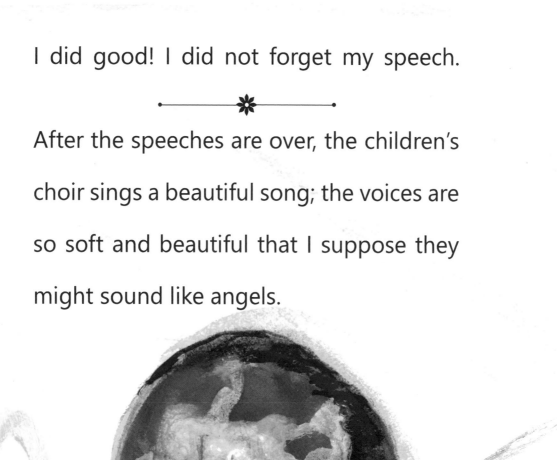

After the speeches are over, the children's choir sings a beautiful song; the voices are so soft and beautiful that I suppose they might sound like angels.

After church service, it is time for the Easter Egg Hunt. It is so much fun! Maybe I'll find the prize egg—the gold one, or one of the plastic eggs with money in it. Oh, how much fun we have at church on Easter Sunday.

You ask, is Easter just a day to get a new dress,

to get new shoes, get your hair done, eat good

food, to say a speech, and hunt Easter Eggs?

No! That's just the fun stuff we do for Easter.

❋

We celebrate Easter because God loved us so much that He sent His son Jesus, who surrendered His life for us; through His surrender and His resurrection, whosoever believes in Him, shall have everlasting life.

That's my Easter Story.

That's what Easter means to me.

Write Your Easter Story

Write an Easter Poem

Add Photos or
Pictures of Your Easter Story

Color the Easter Egg Basket

CPSIA information can be obtained at www.ICGtesting.com
Printed in the USA
BVIW12n0641020617
485817BV00002B/5